My dear mouse friends,

Have I ever told you how much I love science fiction? I've always wanted to write incredible adventures set in another dimension, but I've never believed that parallel universes exist . . . until now!

That's because my good friend Professor Paws von Volt, the brilliant, secretive scientist, has just made an incredible discovery. Thanks to some mousetropic calculations, he determined that there are many different dimensions in time and space, where anything could be possible.

The professor's work inspired me to write this science fiction adventure in which my family and I travel through space in search of new worlds. We're a fabumouse crew: the spacemice!

I hope you enjoy this intergalactic adventure!

Geronimo Stilton

PROFESSOR PAWS VON VOLT

THE SPACEMICE

GERONIMO STILTONIX

TRAP STILTONIX

THEA STILTONIX

GRANDFATHER WILLIAM STILTONIX

ROBOTIX

BENJAMIN STILTONIX AND BUGSY WUGSY

Geronimo Stilton

SPACEMICE

THE UNDERWATER PLANET

Scholastic Inc.

Copyright © 2014 by Edizioni Piemme S.p.A., Palazzo Mondadori, Via Mondadori 1, 20090 Segrate, Italy. International Rights © Atlantyca S.p.A. English translation © 2016 by Atlantyca S.p.A.

The publisher does not have any control over and does not assume any responsibility for author or third-party websites or their content.

GERONIMO STILTON names, characters, and related indicia are copyright, trademark, and exclusive license of Atlantyca S.p.A. All rights reserved. The moral right of the author has been asserted.

Based on an original idea by Elisabetta Dami. www.geronimostilton.com

Published by Scholastic Inc., *Publishers since 1920*, 557 Broadway, New York, NY 10012. SCHOLASTIC and associated logos are trademarks and/or registered trademarks of Scholastic Inc.

Stilton is the name of a famous English cheese. It is a registered trademark of the Stilton Cheese Makers' Association. For more information, go to www.stiltoncheese.com.

No part of this publication may be reproduced, stored in a retrieval system, or transmitted in any form or by any means, electronic, mechanical, photocopying, recording, or otherwise, without written permission of the copyright holder. For information regarding permission, please contact: Atlantyca S.p.A., Via Leopardi 8, 20123 Milan, Italy; e-mail foreignrights@atlantyca.it, www.atlantyca.com.

This book is a work of fiction. Names, characters, places, and incidents are either the product of the author's imagination or are used fictitiously, and any resemblance to actual persons, living or dead, business establishments, events, or locales is entirely coincidental.

ISBN 978-0-545-87243-0

Text by Geronimo Stilton
Original title *Il mistero del pianeta sommerso*
Cover by Flavio Ferron
Illustrations by Giuseppe Facciotto (design) and Daniele Verzini (color)
Graphics by Marta Lorini

Special thanks to AnnMarie Anderson
Translated by Anna Pizzelli
Interior design by Kevin Callahan / BNGO Books

12 11 10 9 8 7 6 5 4 3 2 1   16 17 18 19 20

Printed in the U.S.A.   40

First printing 2016

In the darkness of the farthest galaxy in time and space is a spaceship inhabited exclusively by mice.

This fabumouse vessel is called the **MouseStar 1**, and I am its captain!

I am Geronimo Stiltonix, a somewhat accident-prone mouse who (to tell you the truth) would rather be writing novels than steering a spaceship.

But for now, my adventurous family and I are busy traveling around the universe on exciting intergalactic missions.

THIS IS THE LATEST ADVENTURE OF THE SPACEMICE!

A Rare Day Off!

It all started **early** one morning. I woke up feeling FABUMOUSE! Of course I would have loved to stay in bed for another hour or two. In fact, given the chance, I would *snuggle* under the covers until midday!

What a good night's sleep!

But I was up earlier than usual for a good reason. Oh, I'm so sorry! I almost forgot to introduce myself! My name is Stiltonix, **Geronimo Stiltonix**, and I'm the captain of the *MouseStar 1*, the most mouserific spaceship in the universe. (Honestly, though, my secret dream is to be a world-famouse writer!)

As I was saying, I had asked my **personal assistant robot**, Assistatrix, to wake me up early that morning. I was planning to enjoy a rare day off at *MouseStar 1*'s mousetastic **space beach**. Even the captain deserves a little rest and relaxation every once in a while, don't you think?

So I put on my bathing suit instead of my captain's uniform, and I double-checked my bag to be sure I had all the **ESSENTIALS** . . .

Massaging flip-flops

Sun-shading hat

Self-drying towel

Snorkeling mask

Massaging flip-flops . . . check!

Sun-shading **hat** . . . here!

Self-drying towel . . . got it!

S N O R K E L I N G mask . . . there it is!

Floating beach umbrella . . . yep!

Digital sunglasses . . . hmmm . . . where were they?

I couldn't find them anywhere! Where could they be? Oh yes, how embarrassing! They were right on top of my head!

I was ready to go.

"Beach, here I come!" I cried happily. Then I opened my cabin door and . . . **bang!**

Floating beach umbrella

I bumped right into my cousin Trap.

"Wow, Cousin!" he said in **surprise**. "What are you doing up so early?"

"N-nothing special," I mumbled quickly.

Trap gave me a look. "Oh, really?" he said skeptically. "Then why are you DRESSED like that?"

"W-well, I w-was . . ." I stuttered.

My cousin pulled one of my FLIP-FLOPS out from the top of my bag.

"Don't tell me you're going to the beach without **inviting** any of your family or friends?!" he said.

Black holey galaxies, he had figured it out! Now what was I going to do? Don't get me wrong: I really **love** my cousin. But I had been looking forward to **relaxing** on the beach all by myself. I wanted to focus on the new *book* I was writing. With Trap there, I would be forced to play one beach game after another! Sigh.

"Er . . . yes, that's where I'm going," I confessed. What can I say? I'm an honest mouse!

"I knew it!" Trap said **triumphantly**. "But you'll be so **B O R E D** there by yourself. You know what? I'll get my things and come with you!"

To the Beach, Everyone!

In the end, Trap was right: A day at the beach is a lot more **FUN** with good company! So I **called** my nephew Benjamin; his friend Bugsy Wugsy; and my sister, Thea.

When we went by to pick them up, they were all ready to go.

"**Hi, Uncle!**" my sweet nephew exclaimed as he jumped into my arms and gave me an **enormouse** hug. "Thanks for inviting us to go to the beach with you!"

"You're welcome!" I said. "Now we're all here. **Let's go!**"

Benjamin!

Hi, Uncle!

"Not so fast, Cheesebrain," a loud voice called. "You weren't thinking of going to the beach without me, were you?"

It was my grandfather, *William Stiltonix*, *MouseStar 1*'s retired admiral (and the former captain of the ship!).

"H-hello, Grandfather," I stuttered. "I-I thought you hated the beach. You know, the **SUN**, the space sand—"

"Well, you thought **wrong**!" Grandfather interrupted me. "Everyone knows the **ocean** air is good for a mouse my age!"

So we all **squeezed** into an astrotaxi and sped off toward *MouseStar 1*'s very own space beach.

I know it sounds **impossible**, dear reader,

I love the beach!

8

but it's true! The lower part of our spaceship is a natural biosphere that contains various habitats: There are very **tall** mountains, *rainforests*, lakes, and a wide beach with golden sand by a *crystal-clear* ocean!

"It's so **BEAUTIFUL** here!" Thea exclaimed when we arrived at the beach.

"You had an **EXCELLENT** idea this time, Cuz," Trap proclaimed.

"Yes, an excellent idea, Captain," said a voice behind me.

I turned around to see **Sally de Wrench**, *MouseStar 1*'s expert in photon circuitry, hyperspace engines, and stellar energy. In other words, she's our ship's technical **genius**! And she also happens to be the **loveliest** rodent in the entire galaxy.

"I hope I'm not **intruding**," Sally continued. "Thea told me you were coming

From the Encyclopedia Galactica

NATURAL BIOSPHERE

This area of the *MouseStar 1* includes various natural habitats, including an ocean, mountains, a desert, and a lake. It's an ideal place for a fabumouse space vacation!

Catch!

to the beach, so I thought I'd join in the fun."

"No, no," I told Sally, turning as *red* as a space tomato. "It's absolutely no bother at all. It's a **pleasure** to have you with us!"

"Okay, okay, enough talking!" Trap interrupted us. He was dressed from snout to tail in **swimming** gear, complete with a mask and fins. "Everybody in the ocean!"

Then he grabbed my paw and **pulled** me toward the water.

Hope I'm not intruding!

A MYSTERIOUS OBJECT

As you've probably figured out by now, I *love* the beach. There's nothing better than warm sand under my PAWS and the sun on my fur while I clutch a cheese shake with a *floating* umbrella in one paw. **Ahhhh!**

While I enjoy taking a gentle dip in the ocean to cool off, though, there's one thing that's definitely NOT for me: DIVING! But thanks to my cousin Trap, I found myself at the top of a cliff with the ocean **far**, **far, far** below me.

"Come on! JUMP!" Trap said, prodding me from behind.

Sally was watching us from the beach. I

Jump!

didn't want to make a fool of myself.

I leaned out a bit to look at the **sparkling** water. Suddenly, Trap gave me a shove! I flew clumsily off the cliff, belly flopping into the ocean below. **Splash!**

HOW EMBARRASSING!

When I got out of the **water** Trap was busy making fun of me.

"What a flop, Cousin," he teased. "Diving is definitely not your *forte*! Let's play some Frisbix instead."

"**Good idea**," I replied, hoping to make up for my superstellar flop.

But the game turned out to be harder than I *thought*. I tried to throw the FRISBIX disk along the programmed trajectories, but it kept bouncing off course, flipping around by itself, and getting stuck in the sand!

"Hmm," Trap said teasingly. "Maybe Frisbix isn't your forte, either. Maybe you should go help the mouselings build a sand spaceship!"

From the Encyclopedia Galactica
FRISBIX

Frisbix is a favorite game of spacemice at the beach or park. To play, mice throw an indestructible disk made of stellar steel along various trajectories programmed into it. The momentum created by the player's throw determines where and how far the disk flies.

I ignored my cousin and tried throwing the disk again with all my strength. **Wooooosh!** Galactic Gorgonzola! I had flung the disk so hard I was sure it would stay on course now.

"See!" I shouted proudly. "Look how **FAST** that disk is flying!"

Hey, wait a minute — the disk wasn't **stopping**!

Help!

It soared over Trap's head, past Grandfather William (who was sleeping in the **SUN**), and landed right in the sand spaceship that Benjamin and Bugsy Wugsy had just finished building.

What a disaster!

I ran over to the mouselings to apologize. But before I could utter a word, an ear-piercing scream made my **FUR** stand on end.

Huh?!

"Ouuuuchhhh!"

When he'd ducked out of the way of the *flying* Frisbix disk, Trap had stubbed his paw on something in the sand. Sally dug it up to see what it was: a perfectly **smooth** sphere.

"Hmmm," Sally said as she studied the object, a **puzzled** expression on her snout. "This looks like an **alien** object. I'm not familiar with this **material**..."

"Well, why don't we put it aside so nobody else gets **HURT**?" I suggested.

"Ahem." Thea cleared her throat and stared at me.

"What?" I asked. "I don't want any more *injuries*, do you?"

Ouuuuchhhh!

Thea rolled her **EYES** at me.

"Geronimo, you of all mice should know what needs to be done," she continued. "After all, you're our captain! We have to follow the rules of the *MouseStar 1*: When someone finds a **foreign object** on board, the captain must start an immediate **inquiry**."

An inquiry? I was hoping I had misunderstood, but Sally confirmed it.

"It's true, Geronimo," Sally said, a **serious** expression on her snout. "We have to go back to the **control room** and find out what this strange object is."

I sighed. It looked like my **captain's** duties had followed me to the beach. So much for a **relaxing** day off!

CONGRATULATIONS, CAPTAIN!

We all headed back to the control room, where we met **Professor Greenfur**. He's *MouseStar 1*'s official scientist and an **expert** in alien life-forms.

He immediately began testing the strange **sphere**.

"Let's start with a **photonic scan**," Professor Greenfur instructed Hologramix, our onboard computer.

Stellar Swiss cheese — what did that mean? We all watched as a ray of light

Hmm . . . let's take a look!

illuminated the sphere.

Soon the test results appeared on the control room screen.

Identity: Unknown!

"What?!" Professor Greenfur gasped. "But that's **impossible**. Hologramix has always been able to identify a FOREIGN object with a photonic scan."

"Maybe I can open it with my ultrasonic drill," Sally suggested.

She tried using her powerful space tool on

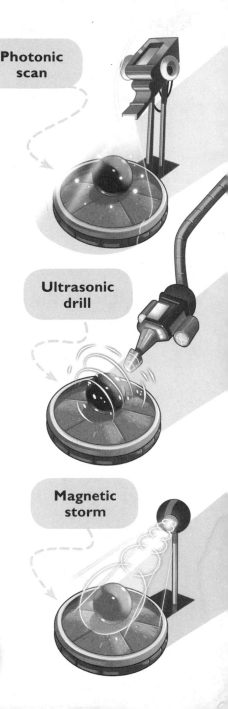

Photonic scan

Ultrasonic drill

Magnetic storm

the sphere, but . . . *nothing* happened! Finally, she gave up.

"I'm sorry," she said apologetically. "It's made of a very **tough** material!"

"There's one last option," Professor Greenfur said. "Unleash the **magnetic storm**!"

But even the magnetic storm didn't work! Professor Greenfur approached me with a **sad** look on his snout.

"Captain, I'm sorry to report that we **CAN'T** figure out what it is!" he said gravely.

"Oh, don't worry," I said reassuringly. "You tried your best."

It was too bad that we hadn't been able to **identify** the object. But at least the inquiry was closed and I could go back to my *vacation day* at the beach!

"Well, I guess that settles it," I began. I was

about to tell everyone they were dismissed when I turned and the *floating* umbrella that was sticking out of my bag bumped the table the sphere was sitting on.

The sphere fell and hit the floor.

Crash!

Solar-smoked Gouda! That thing had almost crushed my tail!

I went to pick it up and put it back in its place when the sphere sent out a puff of **blue smoke**. Then the object began to **rotate**.

My whiskers **trembled** with fear as the sphere continued to spin. Suddenly, **blue**

What in space?

markings appeared on its surface and seemed to be forming words and drawings!

After a few seconds, the sphere slowed to a stop. So I braced myself, picked it up, and saw that the ↑NSCRIPTION was still on its surface. The others were still **squeaking** about ways to open the sphere. They hadn't noticed a thing!

"Um, excuse me," I said slowly, holding out the **strange** blue sphere. "Look at this!"

But no one was paying attention to me.

"**HELLO?!**" I squeaked loudly. "The sphere has been **activated**!"

Everyone turned and stared.

"That's **incredible**!" Trap exclaimed.

"Unbelievable work, Captain!" Sally said. "But how did you do it?"

Sally's praise made me **blush** from the tips of my ears to the end of my tail.

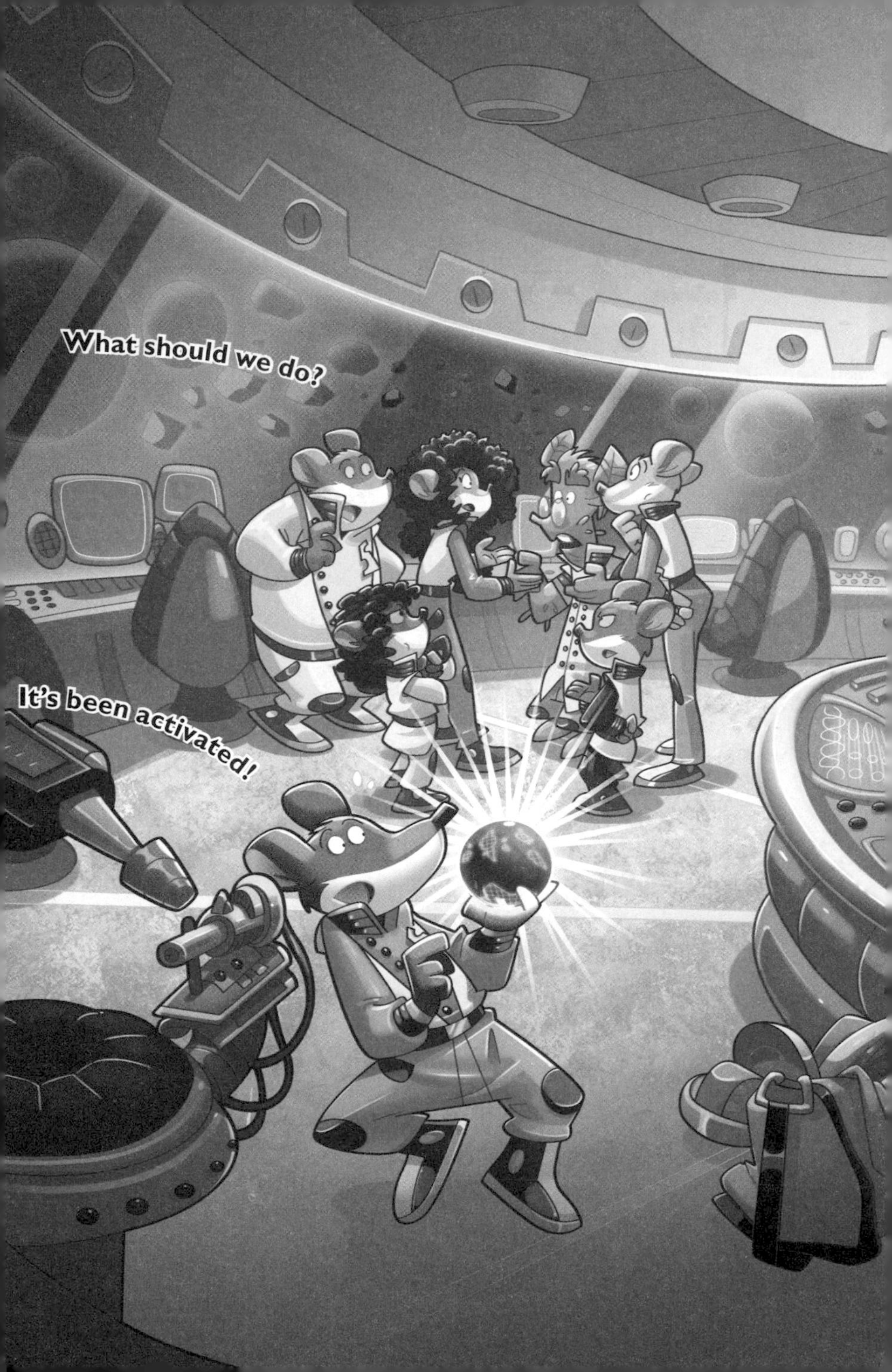
What should we do?
It's been activated!

"Well done, Cuz!" Trap said, slapping me on the back so hard I almost lost my **BALANCE**. "You finally made yourself *useful!*"

Professor Greenfur took the sphere from my paws and studied it *closely*.

"These lines ... two *X*s and some numbers ... H M M M ..." he squeaked to himself softly.

We waited to hear what he had to say.

"There is no doubt about it," he announced a moment later. "It's a **map**!"

I'm Not Cut Out for Adventure!

Benjamin came closer, **LOOKING** excited.

"It's a *treasure map*, isn't it, Uncle?!" he exclaimed, his eyes bright. "We have to plan an **expedition**!"

Oh, Benjamin has such an imagination!

"Benjamin, we don't know what it is," I explained carefully. "And even if it is a treasure map, we don't know where it would lead us. It could be very, very **dangerous** . . ."

"But Professor Greenfur is a fabumouse scientist!" Trap interjected. "I'm sure he can **INTERPRET** the map for us."

"Why, thank you," the professor replied.

AQUARIX

"And now that you mention it, these numbers might be **coordinates** from space."

"That's an interesting hypothesis," Thea agreed. "Let's enter these numbers into the galaxy planetarium map and see what happens."

A second later, an image of the planet Aquarix appeared on the control room screen. There was a large red X in one spot.

"That's where the sphere is from!" Professor Greenfur cried. "**AQUARIX**!"

"But how did it get onto OUR spaceship?" I asked.

"Good question," Professor Greenfur replied. He pressed a few **BUTTONS** on *MouseStar 1*'s control panel computer.

"Ah, I see," he said. "The sand on our beach comes from **Aquarix**!"

"Then this sphere came on board along with the sand!" Thea explained. "We have to take it back to where it came from."

TAKE IT BACK? Martian mozzarella! Something told me a **BiG** adventure was **looming**, and there's nothing I dislike more than adventures!

"B-but 99.99 percent of the surface of Aquarix is covered by **water**, right?" I pointed out. "So what even exists there?"

"Oh, nothing special," Trap replied. "Just some underwater **volcanoes**, deep-sea **monsters**,

Volcanoes?! Monsters?! Fur-eating seaweed?!

and some FUR—EATING seaweed."

W-what? My whiskers **trembled** with fear. There was no way I was even getting close to that planet! Luckily, I knew we didn't have the right equipment for it.

"Well, that sounds like a really fabumouse adventure," I fibbed. "It's just too bad that we don't have the right underwater *navigational* system to travel there."

"Er, Captain?" Sally interrupted. "I actually just finished building an **underwater spaceship**! This would be the perfect opportunity to test it out, don't you agree?"

Stinky space cheese! What had I gotten myself into? I couldn't say **NO** to Sally: It would be too **embarrassing** if she knew what a scaredy-mouse I am!

"Y-yes, of course," I agreed. "I'll just stay behind on the *MouseStar 1* while you go on

From the Encyclopedia Galactica
UNDERWATER SPACESHIP

Infrared super-telescope

Escape pod

Headlights (for seeing into any dark, scary abyss!)

Jet engine

Panoramic porthole

Mechanical forceps

the mission. I have a few **CHORES** to do anyway."

"*Stellar Swiss*, Grandson!" Grandfather William squeaked loudly. "How many times do I have to tell you that the **captain** always has to be present on discovery missions? You must leave with the others immediately!"

Unfortunately, it's impossible for me to argue with Grandfather.

"Y-yes, of course," I **stammered**. "So . . . hm . . . Thea, Trap, and Sally: Let's get ready to leave."

"What about me, Uncle?" Benjamin asked. "Can Bugsy Wugsy and I come on the **treasure hunt**, too? Pretty please with cheese on top?"

I couldn't say **no** to his **SWEET** smile. So I sighed and nodded.

A Fabumouse
Discovery!

And so that's how I found myself traveling to Aquarix in an underwater spaceship with Thea, Sally, Trap, Professor Greenfur, Benjamin, and Bugsy Wugsy. I was trying not to think about the fact that I would soon be underwater. I only like to sit **near** the ocean, not go **UNDER** it!

When Aquarix became visible from our porthole, Trap approached me, a bag of crunchy **blue cheese crusts** in his paw.

"Want some?" he asked as he *crunched* on a mouthful of the snacks. "They're really good!"

"No, thank you," I replied. "I'm not hungry."

"What's up, Cousin?" Trap asked. "You're awfully **quiet**. Don't tell me you're scared?!"

"Wh-who me?" I asked, clearing my throat. "**Of course not!**"

Trap put his arm around my shoulders.

"Look, I was just **kidding** before about the volcanoes, the monsters, and the fur-eating seaweed," he explained. "Just relax! This treasure hunt will be **FUN**!"

"Buckle your seat belts!" Thea announced a moment later. She was at the controls. "*Prepare* to submerge!"

WHOOSH!

With a WHOOSH, the spaceship suddenly sank into the deep waters of Aquarix.

We were all squeakless from the view. We were surrounded by *blue* water, and the alien fish swimming by had the most unique COLORS and **shapes**!

"How *wonderful*!" Sally gasped.

"How **bizarre**!" Benjamin exclaimed as he pointed to a fish with six **eyes**.

Meanwhile, Bugsy Wugsy was snapping photos.

"These will make a great impression at **school** when we study water planets!" she explained.

Professor Greenfur checked the map and we began to **navigate** toward the big **X**.

The trip was turning out better than I had expected. Sally's underwater spaceship was so **comfortable** that I found myself

drifting off to sleep in my comfy captain's chair . . .

Suddenly, I awoke with a start.

"That's it! That's it!" Professor Greenfur **squeaked**. He was pointing to something outside the spaceship.

"What is it?" I asked, still **dazed** from my little ratnap.

"SUPERBOOST SEAWEED!" Professor Greenfur explained enthusiastically. "It's been a few cosmic years since I saw a specimen. It's an **extremely rare** seaweed with exceptional nutritional properties. We absolutely **must** collect a sample for my research!"

"Of course!" I agreed.

Professor Greenfur

was a true expert in **inTeRGaLacTic BoTanY**, and I knew finding a rare species in a hidden corner of our galaxy was very **important** to him!

Thea slowly maneuvered our vessel close to the seabed. Then Sally used the ship's external mechanical forceps to pick two **tiny** sprigs of the precious seaweed. She was very careful not to damage the plant.

A Squeaky-Clean Getaway

A moment later, the entire spaceship began to SHAKE.

"Wh-what was that?" I asked Thea.

"Something seems to have hit us," my sister explained calmly.

Then a second, stronger TREMOR struck. I lost my balance and almost crashed to the floor of the ship!

"Uncle, what's going on?" Benjamin asked with a shaky voice.

I looked out the porthole. Holey craters! Enormouse *green* tendrils were wrapped around the outside of our spaceship!

"Oh no!" Professor Greenfur said

desperately. "It's fierce fur-eating seaweed, the **deadliest** seaweed species in the universe."

Martian mozzarella! We were *doomed*!

The underwater spaceship continued to shake as we **BOUNCED** around inside it.

"I thought you told me you were *kidding* about the fur-eating seaweed!" I yelled at Trap.

"Well, it was meant to be a *joke*, but I guess I got it right!" Trap shouted.

But my brave, **fearless** sister didn't back down. Thea tried to break free of the tendrils with a few fancy **maneuvers**, but the plant's hold on our ship just got tighter and tighter. So Sally used the mechanical forceps to cut pieces of the plant . . . but the more she cut, the more the seaweed grew back and *twisted* around us!

After a few minutes, we heard some **FRIGHTENING** sounds:

Scrick . . . screek . . . scraaaak!

Galactic Gouda! The tightening *seaweed* was breaking our spaceship apart!

"There's nothing else to do!" Thea explained. "If I **BLAST** the engines, I might make the situation worse."

"We're running out of time!" Sally exclaimed. "If we don't do something soon, we'll all be seaweed food!"

The next tremor caused an enormouse spaceship **instruction manual** to fall on my head.

BONK!

Ouch! I leaned over to get it, and saw it was open to a page on spaceship maintenance. Not knowing what else to do, I began reading aloud.

"Cleaning the spaceship with stellar soap . . ." I muttered. Of course — soap! "Sally, start the auto-cleaning cycle!"

I crossed my paws and hoped it would work. In less than a second, the spaceship was covered with a **special** ultra-cleaning soap. The sudsy bubbles made the surface of the spaceship very, very **slippery**.

The seaweed slipped right off the spaceship. Thea **blasted** the engines

and we got out of there
immediately.

We were free!

We all cheered and
hugged.

"Uncle G, you
were **amazing**!"
Benjamin cried.

"It was just luck,"
I said modestly.

Suddenly, the **inside** of the spaceship was full of **soap bubbles**. Giant brushes scrubbed everything from top to bottom, including the crew!

"The auto-cleaning cycle covers both the exterior and the **interior** of the spaceship," Sally explained as two enormouse brushes rolled over my fur. Oops! At least it was just soap. Finally, a strong squirt of **warm air** dried us off and fluffed our fur.

Thankful to be safe (and **squeaky-clean!**), we continued with our expedition.

ATTACK OF THE PIRANHAX

I had just leaned back in my chair to relax and admire the underwater **scenery** outside the porthole window when the control panel began beeping.

BEEP... **BEEP...** BEEP... **BEEP...** **BEEP!**

"What's going on now, Thea?" I asked.

"It looks like we're heading toward a swarm of . . . something!" she replied.

Sally activated the **infrared super-telescope.**

"It's a **SWARM** of fishoids! And they're heading toward **US!**"

My whiskers **TREMBLED** with fear.

"Calm down, Geronimo," Trap said.

"What could be worse than the **fur-eating seaweed**?"

Professor Greenfur turned to us, a **serious** look on his snout.

"Let's not underestimate the dangers of the underwater world," he warned us.

Meanwhile, Sally had connected the telescope to the control panel computer screen. A weird alien fish appeared on the screen. It was tiny but had very SHARP teeth!

"I knew it!" the professor exclaimed. "They're bigteeth piranhax! These fishoid creatures will eat pretty much anything that's in their way. They are extremely dangerous. We absolutely must avoid them!"

Thea didn't waste a second more. With a sudden turn, she wedged the spaceship between some sand dunes. We all held our breath, waiting for the **piranhax** to pass by. Sally peered through the telescope again.

"Well done, Thea!" Sally cheered. "We **lost** them!"

We all **squeaked** with joy.

"Uh-oh," Benjamin said, pointing out the porthole. "Maybe we're celebrating too soon."

Sally aimed the headlights into the abyss ahead, **illuminating** dozens . . . no, hundreds . . . no, THOUSANDS of hungry **PIRANHAX**! And they were lined up in a very threatening attack formation!

What had I done to **deserve** this? All I wanted was a nice, quiet **vacation day** at the beach. And now I was stuck on

an underwater spaceship, about
to be eaten alive by alien fishoids!

But as usual, my sister would not give up.

"I'll show them what I'm made of!" she
shouted. "HOLD ON TIiiiiiiIGHT!"

Thea powered up the engines and the
spaceship **took off**. She executed a few
very fast and unpredictable maneuvers.
There were **twists**, abrupt stops, and a
sudden change of **direction**. My stomach
lurched up and down and from side to side. I
thought I was going to *toss my cheese*!

But every time we thought we had **lost** them, the piranhax would reappear in **hot pursuit**.

AN ESCAPE PLAN

After what seemed like the twentieth failed maneuver, Trap was ready to throw in the towel.

"We'll never lose them," he groaned. "They're **too fast**!"

But Benjamin suddenly had an idea.

"Wait!" he said. "At school we studied the behavior of sea aliens in a swarm. They will always follow a **SINGLE TARGET**. If we manage to direct their attention to something else, we might be able to get away!"

"But **HOW** do we do that?" Bugsy asked. "We would need a second spaceship."

"We have the **escape pod**!" Sally exclaimed. Then she explained her plan. "We'll slip behind a rock and then we'll launch the

Here's the plan! escape pod. Once the piranhax change course, Thea will accelerate to maximum speed and we'll leave the **deadly** fishoids behind!"

"Great idea!" Professor Greenfur agreed.

But I was **worried**.

"If we launch the escape pod, we'll be left without it," I reminded everyone.

"Cousin, do you hear that noise?" Trap asked.

CLICK   CLICK   CLICK   CLICK   CLICK   CLICK

CLICK   CLICK   CLICK   CLICK   CLICH

"Yes . . ." I said hesitantly.

"That's the CLICKING of piranhax teeth!" Trap continued, his squeak getting higher. "Would you rather become **fish food**?"

"No!" I said, coming to my senses. We didn't have a choice: We had to sacrifice the escape pod if we wanted **to survive**! "Let's implement the plan!"

"**Buckle up**, everyone," Thea said. We took our seats and Thea guided the spaceship as **QUICKLY** as it would go,

squeezing into a NARROW space between two rocks.

The piranhax were disoriented. It was the PERFECT moment to carry out our plan!

Sally launched the escape pod, which shot far away. Thea turned the engines off so the piranhax wouldn't **hear** us.

In the meantime, I squeezed my eyes shut in fear.

SWISHHHHHHH!

The sound of the water above our heads could only mean one thing: The swarm of piranhax had rushed past us, following the escape pod! The plan had worked!

MORE TROUBLE!

Once we had escaped, Professor Greenfur consulted the map.

"I have good news," he told us. "According to the map, we're halfway there!"

Only halfway? Was he kidding?!

The trip was turning out to be much more **DANGEROUS** than I had imagined. Our ship had almost been **crushed** by fur-eating seaweed tendrils, and then a school of deadly piranhax had almost turned us into fish food! Not to mention the fact that we were who-knows-how-far below the surface of the ocean on an alien planet . . .

I **shuddered**. How could we be just **halfway** through this fur-raising mission? Maybe focusing on my **SWEET** nephew

Benjamin and his friend Bugsy Wugsy would help keep me from **panicking**.

For a short while, I was able to relax as we played a game of I Spy. But when Sally interrupted us, I knew it was **BAD** news.

"Captain, we have a problem," Sally said. Oh no, not again! I did my best to remain **cool**, calm, and collected.

"What is it?" I asked.

Sally showed me the control dashboard, which was covered in little flashing **red lights**.

"Take a look for yourself, Captain," she replied. I stared at the *screen*, but I was out of my league. I didn't have a **clue** what was happening!

"Hmmm," I murmured sheepishly. "Maybe you can explain it to me."

"These signals indicate **breakdowns**

that need to be fixed right away," Sally explained kindly. "Otherwise we won't be able to continue with the mission!"

Martian mozzarella! Breakdowns? That's all we needed!

"The spacecraft was **weakened** by the seaweed tentacles, and the maneuvers to escape the piranhax have made things worse!" Sally continued. "We have to stop as soon as possible to make the repairs."

Professor Greenfur pointed to a *dark*

Underwater helmet

Navigational backpack (with minirockets!)

All-purpose, fix-everything drill

opening in front of us.

"We could take shelter in that underwater **cave**!" he said.

"Yes — according to radar, it's **empty**," Thea agreed. Then she **gently** steered our ship into the shelter.

Sally wasted no time. She put on her underwater helmet and grabbed the special navigational **backpack** (complete with minirockets). And of course she took her all-purpose, fix-everything **drill**, which was another one of her **useful** inventions!

At that moment, Trap jumped to his paws.

"I'll go with you," he said.

"I really need to stretch my **paws**! But you should stay here, Cuz. After all, someone needs to keep Benjamin and Bugsy Wugsy company."

Solar-smoked Gouda! Trap was going to make me look like a real wimp in Sally's eyes. I sighed. Even though I was completely scared to go out and explore that dark cave, I knew I had to do it. Before Sally and Trap were out of the ship, I had pulled on a helmet and a backpack, too.

"Wait for me!" I squeaked. "I'm coming with you!"

THE BELLY OF THE BEAST

The cave was much darker than it had appeared from inside the spaceship. We **turned on** our helmet headlights, which illuminated the bright red cave walls. I touched one to find that it was strangely **soft**. It almost felt like a mattress!

Trap was swimming around as if he was on a scuba-diving vacation while Sally was busy fixing the spaceship's external computer **SCREEN** with her drill.

"Hey, come here, Geronimo!" I heard Trap shout through his helmet **microphone**. "It's super **soft**!"

But I couldn't see my cousin **anywhere**!

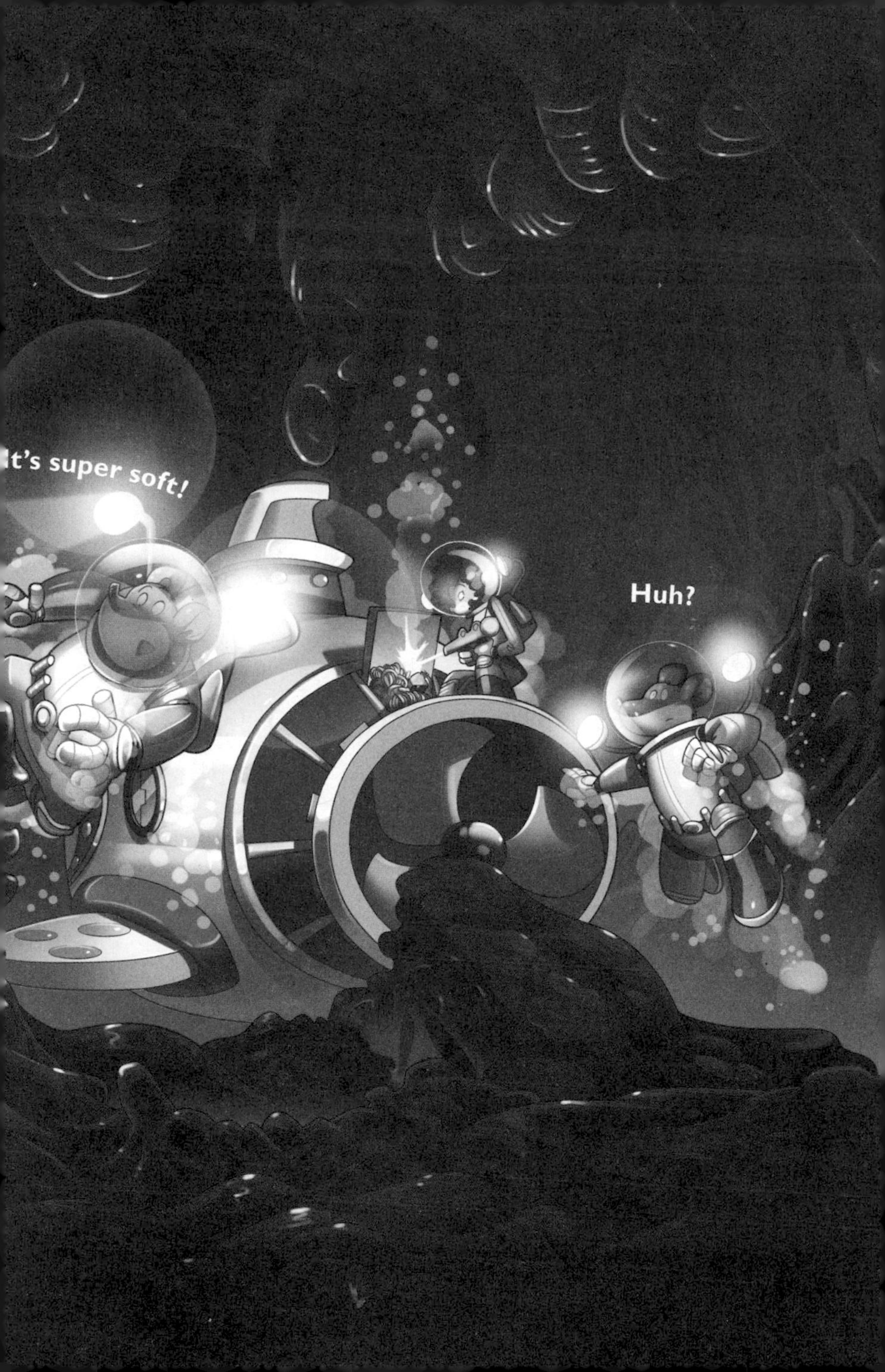
It's super soft!
Huh?

"I can't find you, Trap . . . **It's too dark!**" I replied. I tried my best to remain calm, but my teeth were chattering with fright.

"I'm almost done," Sally updated us through her helmet's microphone. "Just another minute."

I turned around so I could start going back toward the mouth of the cave, but it was very *DIFFICULT* to move through the water in the **dark**. Somehow, I found myself **UPSIDE DOWN**!

As if that wasn't enough, a strong current suddenly **KNOCKED** me over. I grabbed a piece of sea coral and hung on for dear life, hoping I wouldn't be dragged away!

"Everything okay, G?" Trap asked. I was about to answer when I was interrupted by an enormouse **roar**.

RRRROOOOAAAARRRR!

Black holey galaxies! What was that? The water around me started **churning** and I was tossed from left to right. Thank goodmouse I had found that **coral** to hold on to!

"Come back to the ship right away!" Thea called into our helmets from a microphone in the command room.

"Geronimo!" Trap's voice squeaked in my helmet. "We have to go!"

"I can't make it!" I replied. "I'm holding on to some coral and if I let go, I don't know where I'll **end up**!"

"Okay, I'll come get you!" Trap replied.

A moment later, Trap was at my side. But I still couldn't let go: I was too **afraid**! So Trap began to **PULL ME** with all his strength. The more he pulled, the more the cave **shook** and the louder the **scary** howl became.

AAAAAHHHHUUUUUUU!

Eventually, with all that pulling, the coral I was holding on to **snapped**. A moment later, we were all floating in the **water** toward the spaceship. And, strangely, the trembling of

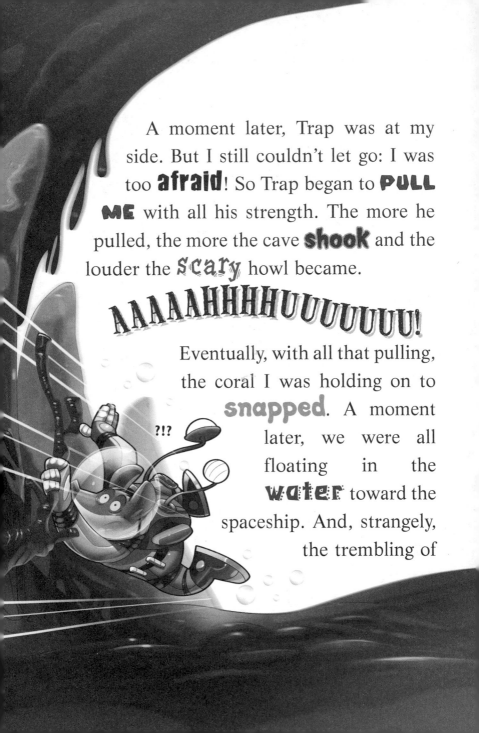

?!?

the cave and the **SCARY** howling had stopped!

Once we got back inside the spaceship, we took off our helmets and backpacks. **"Are you ok, Uncles?"** a scared Benjamin asked me and Trap.

"We're fine," I assured him. Now that I was back inside, I was feeling a little **calmer**. "But we'd better get out of here soon. I don't want to feel another underwater earthquake in this lifetime!"

"Yes, we should go," Thea agreed. "And we should do it quickly, because the **cave** entrance is closing!"

"Wh-what?" I exclaimed. "How can it be **c-closing**?"

Suddenly, I realized what was happening.

We were not in a cave!

A Thorny Issue

Thea **pushed** the engines to their limits and managed to guide the spaceship out right before the cave entrance — or what *seemed* to be a cave entrance — **snapped** shut.

"Are you thinking what I'm thinking?" I asked everyone.

"Yup," Trap replied. "We just came through some really **G I A N T** teeth!"

"Then we were in the мoυтн of a giant sea creature?!" Benjamin asked, incredulous.

"Exactly!" Professor Greenfur confirmed as he glanced back at the giant beast through the porthole. "We were inside an enormouse **Silverix whale**!"

"And why didn't you let us know this

earlier, Professor?" Thea objected, her paws on her hips.

"I didn't notice," Professor Greenfur replied. "The whale had perfectly CAMOUFLAGED himself to look like a cave. I imagine he was trying to attract prey!"

"Yeah — us!" Trap chimed in. He peered out the porthole. "What's he doing now?"

The WHALE had started moving toward us.

"He thinks we're food and wants to EAT us!" I squeaked at the top of my lungs. "This time, we're done for!"

"Full speed ahead, Thea!" Sally shouted.

"We're already at top speed!" my sister replied.

The creature caught up to us in three shakes of a whale's tail.

But to our great surprise, he didn't slurp us up in one GULP. Instead he lifted a

gigantic fin in front of his **eyes** and let out a strange whistle: **Fiiiiuuuuuuiiiii!**

"It seems like he wants to tell us something," Bugsy Wugsy mused.

"Let's activate the translator I installed to be able to understand alien languages," Sally suggested.

But I was **suspicious**.

"A-are you really sure?" I asked. "It could be a setup . . ."

"Uncle, look at those **big, sweet eyes**!" Benjamin remarked trustingly. And to be honest, if Benjamin wasn't **afraid**, why should I be?

Sally's device began the translation:

"My name is Lucas. Thank you for pulling the thorn from my throat!"

We all looked at one another, dumbfounded. What thorn was the whale talking about?

But then Trap understood.

"Of course!" he realized. "He's talking about what you thought was a piece of coral, Geronimo. When I pulled you, it was dislodged from the whale's mouth."

I stepped up to the **microphone**.

"It's very nice to meet you, Lucas," I replied. "We are **SPACEMICE**, and we're happy we were able to help you!"

"I'll always owe you, spacemice!" he replied. "**Bon voyage!**"

We waved from the porthole and the whale winked back at us before he disappeared into the abyss. We had finally made a **friend** on the strange underwater planet of Aquarix!

An Underwater City

Galactic Gorgonzola, this had been a really difficult trip! Luckily, the map was showing that we were getting closer to our destination. Thea *guided* the spaceship over a steep reef, around an underwater **mountain** with sharp peaks, and through a narrow canyon. Finally we reached the point that was marked by an **X** on the map.

A **beautiful** city came into view.

"It's so pretty," Benjamin said. "But it's also so **DARK**!"

It's true — the few lights in the city seemed to barely **illuminate** the houses and streets.

Thea gently landed the spaceship outside

the gates to the city.

"We're finally here!" Trap announced. "Come on, everyone. Let's go! I can't wait to see if there really is a †reasure. Then we can get back to the 𝖬𝗈𝗎𝗌𝖾𝖲𝗍𝖺𝗋 1. Boy, do I miss Cook Squizzy's lunar cheese fondue!"

I had no desire to get out of the spaceship again, but I knew I had to. So I reluctantly pulled on my helmet and headed for the door.

"I'll wait on the ship," Thea said. "And we'll **keep in touch** through the helmet microphones."

 **1. Here I go!**

Sally was already standing by the door, lining everyone up.

"Here we go!" she announced briskly. "Professor Greenfur and I will go last. Trap — **OUT**! Benjamin and Bugsy Wugsy — **OUT**! Captain Geronimo Stiltonix — **OUT**!"

2.
Ha, ha, ha!

3. Oof!

As soon as I stepped outside, I immediately flipped **UPSIDE DOWN** in the murky water. It took me a while to **flip** back over and join the others, so I was the last one to arrive at the gate to the underwater city.

"Finally, Captain!" Trap said, rolling his eyes at me. "Now what do we do?"

"I don't know," I replied. "Knock?"

No one objected, so I reached out a paw and knocked three times:

Knock! Knock! Knock!

MASTERS OF THE LIGHT

A few moments later, the door opened. Some small, friendly-looking **blue** aliens greeted us. Each alien had **FOUR** eyes, *eight* tentacles, and some unusual PIPES on its head. Tiny **bubbles** streamed out of the pipes.

"This would be a good time to introduce yourselves," Thea reminded us through our helmet microphones.

Trap **pushed** me forward.

"It's your turn, Captain!" he whispered.

Me? Why, oh why is it always **me**? Oh, right . . . because I'm the **captain**!

"Hello! We are **spacemice**," I told the aliens. "We come in peace!"

"Nice to meet you!" one of the aliens replied. "We are POLPYX. Welcome to Aquarix City, our capital! If you follow us, we'll take you to our *wise ones*!"

"And who are these wise ones?" I asked hesitantly. I hoped they were friendly, too!

"They are our three Masters of the Light."

Masters of the Light? What in the cosmos were they?

We had no other choice but to follow the polpyx, so we swam after them along the city's **dark** streets. As we passed each little house, other polpyx came

Follow me!

out to say **hello**.

"What nice, **friendly** aliens," Benjamin remarked. "I could do a **paper** about this planet for school!"

"That's a **great** idea!" I agreed.

We soon arrived in a small **underwater** cavern. The wise ones were three polpyx with **thick white beards**. Each one held a long stick topped by a small, **shiny** star.

The wise ones slowly rose and *swam* toward us. The polpyx that had led us to the cavern whispered something to one of the wise ones. The alien nodded his head.

"Hello, spacemice!" the wise one said in a **WELCOMING** tone. "We are happy to have you visit. We are a friendly species."

Then he stopped and another wise one took over.

"We have been living at the bottom of the sea for **thousands** of years," the second alien said in a voice that was *lower* than the first alien's. "We like to meet new friends from **faraway places**."

Finally, the third wise one spoke. His voice was the **lowest** of all of them.

"Yes, you are most welcome here in **AQUARIX CITY**," he agreed. "But please do tell us what brought you all the way down here to the **dark** abyss."

Before I could reply, Trap stepped forward.

"Excuse me, Captain," he whispered in my ear. "Mind if I speak? Otherwise we'll never get through these pleasantries, and I'm *STARVING*!"

Before I could protest, my cousin grabbed the **sphere** with the map from Professor Greenfur's paws and showed it to the polpyx.

"This sphere brought us here!" he announced.

It was the sphere!

A Secret Key

When they saw the sphere, the three aliens were **speechless**. After a moment of silence, they finally spoke:

"I-I . . ."

"C-can't . . ."

"B-believe it!"

Then they began chattering quickly among themselves, IGNORING us completely!

Finally, the creatures turned back to us.

"Oh, please *forgive* us," the first one said.

"We thought this sphere had disappeared forever!" the second one added.

"The last time we saw it was three lunar cycles ago, just before the **great tsunami**!" the third one concluded.

"How did you find it?" they asked in unison.

"Well, it happened to be on our **SPACESHIP**," I replied.

"After we **activated** it, we decided to follow the map," Professor Greenfur explained. "We wanted to find out where the sphere had **come from**!"

The wise ones smiled widely.

"We are extremely grateful to you for this, spacemice!" the first wise one said. "This isn't just a map — it's also the secret key to the **Light chest**!"

I didn't have a clue what they were **SQUEAKING** about!

The wise ones began mumbling among themselves again.

"Did you understand any of that?" I asked Professor Greenfur.

"I think so," he murmured. "The stars on top of the sticks they're carrying look like extremely rare **marine cosmostars**. They are packed with **energy** that helps plants grow in really **DARK** places like this city. Maybe the light chest has something to do with that."

The second wise one turned back to us.

"That's **correct**!" the alien said. "Our civilization has been able to grow down here in the dark abyss thanks to the marine cosmostars."

"But we only have a few cosmostars left," the first alien added. "And it's extremely difficult and dangerous to find new ones!"

"Our ancestors hid an emergency supply of cosmostars in a special chest," the third alien explained. "They wanted to keep our civilization from using them all up RIGHT AWAY. But we thought the key to the chest had been lost **forever**!"

So the strange blue sphere really was a treasure map! And the treasure was very **precious** to these aliens and their entire underwater civilization.

"Spacemice, we trust you," the first wise one said. "Follow us!"

The wise ones **ILLUMINATED** the way with their *sticks*, and we followed them toward a tall, **dark** building.

A **CHILL** ran down my tail. The polpyx seemed friendly, but

Follow us!

I was afraid of the unknown. I turned to Benjamin and Bugsy.

"This could be **dangerous**," I told the little mice. "Why don't you two wait here?" Benjamin was a little disappointed, but two young polpyx came up to us and began to play with him and Bugsy Wugsy right away.

I waved good-bye and entered the tall building with the others.

What fun!

UNEXPECTED VISITORS

We followed the Masters of the Light all the way to a great hall.

"There it is!" the second wise one exclaimed, pointing to a **big chest** in the center of the room.

As soon as we got closer to the chest, the sphere began to shine!

"The sphere is letting us know that we have reached the ultimate destination," the first wise one explained.

We all stepped closer to the chest, **eager** to see what was inside.

"Let's hurry up and open it!" Trap said impatiently. "I'm so curious, and my tummy's really **grumbling**!"

Then he stepped up to the chest and

placed the sphere in one of the two round openings in the middle.

We all held our breath, waiting to hear the **clicking** sound of the lock. Instead, the chest projected a **blue ray of light** that spelled out this message:

"The chest of light will open for you. Just place the second sphere here, too!"

The wise ones shook their heads.

"There are two keys!" the third one said. "Our ancestors created **two** spheres, but both were **lost**!"

We were all disappointed.

"Then we came all this way for NOTHING?" Sally asked sadly.

Before anyone could reply, we heard a cackle behind us.

"Oh, this is going to be good!"

We all turned around.

Black holey galaxies: It was **Black Star**, captain of the **Pirate Spacecats**!

How did I recognize him, you might ask? It's simple: Every mouse in the **Cheddar Galaxy** knows about the terrible pirate spacecats and their ruthless captain, Black Star. Plus, he has a **big black star** on his forehead! The pirate spacecats love to invade different planets and steal whatever **precious** treasures they can find. They're **feared** across the galaxy!

I tried to contact Thea immediately. But my helmet **microphone** seemed to be on mute.

"Don't even THiNK about trying to contact your **spaceship**, Captain," Black Star growled into my ear. "It's no use."

Then he motioned to a particularly vicious-looking member of his crew. The spacecat brought in someone who looked very *familiar*: It was Thea, and she was TIED up!

MOUSEY METEORITES!

The pirates had captured her!

BLACK STAR
Captain of the pirate spacecats

Species: **Feline**

Specialty: **Attacking alien planets to hunt for riches and treasures**

Characteristics: **He's cold-blooded, but has aristocratic manners.**

Defining Features: **A black star on his forehead and foul breath that stinks like moldy sardines**

How Should
I Put It?

"Let her go right now, you putrid and pugnacious pirates!" Trap shouted.

"Huh?" asked the spacecat.

Black Star rolled his eyes.

"He wants you to **release** the prisoner," he told his crew member. Then he turned to Trap. "There's no need to yell big words. We didn't come to this awful planet to get our tails wet with you, spacemice. Let her go, Galaxia!"

As soon as the spacecat untied her, Thea filled us in on what had happened.

"Those pirates took me by complete

surprise," she explained. "I didn't have time to sound the **ALARM**. And I'm afraid they may have d̶e̶s̶t̶r̶o̶y̶e̶d̶ our spaceship!"

"Quiet!" Black Star growled. Then he reached into his bag for something.

Holey craters, what was that? A lunar laser? A stellar space sword? A meteorite slingshot?

I covered my eyes with my paws. *Good-bye, universe!* I thought.

Thank goodmouse I was wrong: Black Star pulled out **the second sphere**!

"Were you looking for this?" he asked with a sneer.

The wise ones were s̶h̶o̶c̶k̶e̶d̶.

"H-how did you get that?" the third one asked.

Looking for this?

"Calm down, calm down, no need to get **excited**," Black Star began. "The story is SIMPLE: I was returning from one of our — how should I put it? — one of our sightseeing voyages . . ."

At that, the other spacecats **burst out** laughing.

"Ha, ha, ha!" they chuckled. "Sightseeing! That's a good one, Captain!"

"QUiET!" Black Star yowled. "How many times do I have to tell you not to interrupt me?"

The four pirates immediately quieted down.

"Now, where was I?" Black Star continued. "Ah, yes. We were coming back from a voyage in the galaxy and I was going through all the objects that the nice aliens we met had — how should I put it? — *given* to us . . ."

"Ha, ha, ha!" the spacecats burst out. "**Given** to us! Where do you come up with such funny **JOKES**, Captain?"

"**Quiiieeet!**" Black Star roared again. "The next one who meows without authorization will stay here underwater — **forever!**"

Trembling with fear, the four pirates quieted down again.

"As I was saying," Black Star continued, "I found this **MYSTERIOUS** sphere among the various objects we had collected. I didn't know what it was, but the other day it suddenly started to **shine**. It revealed a map that led the way to *Aquarix*, and now here we are!"

"Of course!" Professor Greenfur exclaimed. "When Captain Stiltonix activated our sphere, the *second* sphere was activated as well!"

"Do you mean the spheres are designed to force the owners of each object to meet up?" Trap asked.

"Yes, exactly!" Professor Greenfur confirmed. "And the two spheres have to come together in order to open the chest."

"Well said, spacemouse!" Black Star said. He extended his **PAW**, and his SHARP claws glistened in the seawater. Then he tapped poor Professor Greenfur's helmet.

Click! Click! Click!

"Now **please** tell me, what do I need to do to open this chest?" he asked with a polite growl.

Professor Greenfur shook like a leaf.

"I . . . w-well . . . s-so . . ." the professor stuttered.

Then the first wise one **spoke** up.

"Place the second sphere . . ."

"In the second opening . . ." the second wise one continued.

"And the chest will open!" concluded the third wise one.

"Thank you, little aliens!" Black Star purred happily. He knew it didn't hurt to use **good manners**, even if he was **stealing** something that didn't belong to him!

GRAB THE TREASURE!

All we could do was watch the pirate insert the sphere into the chest.

clack!

The key clicked into place and the chest opened up.

A **blinding** light lit up the room. Black Star had to cover his eyes with his **paw** as he peered inside.

"Mouse skulls and fish bones!" he exclaimed happily. "There are dozens of **cosmostars** in here! I'll sell these all over the galaxy, and then I'll be **rich**!"

Then he turned to his crew.

"Come on, **Galaxia**," Black Star said to one of the pirates. "Get moving, **flea face**. Grab the treasure and load it onto our spaceship."

Then he gave the rest of us a threatening look.

"If you stay here quietly, I'll leave you alone," he hissed menacingly. "I won't pull a **single** hair out of your fur before I leave with the treasure. But if you try to stop me . . ."

"Th-then what?" I asked, my whiskers **trembling**.

He showed off his SHaRP, ShiNy claws.

I'll be rich!

"Then you can kiss your fur **good-bye**, spacemice!"

No one had the COURAGE to move a muscle. But even if we had been brave enough to try to stop the pirates, what could we have done? The citizens of Aquarix were **peaceful** creatures, and there were many more spacecats than there were spacemice. We had to SAVE OUR FUR!

The treasure is ours!

Let's go!

So we watched helplessly as the pirates loaded the *big* chest onto a trailer that was tied to their **spaceship**.

Just before he closed the door to the spaceship, Black Star turned back to us.

"Oh, how RUDE of me!" he purred. "I almost forgot to thank you! It was a *pleasure* doing business with you. Hope to see you all again soon! Ha, ha, ha, ha, ha!"

Then the spaceship door slid closed and the spacecats took off in a swirl of *bubbles* and sand.

The wise ones were **devastated**.

"Our **precious** cosmostars!" the first one moaned.

"They are lost forever," the second one said sadly.

"What are we going to do now?" the third one asked.

I felt **AWFUL**. We had been so close to helping the polpyx get their cosmostars back, but instead we had unwittingly led the pirates right to the **TREASURE**!

As we watched the pirates' spaceship **ZOOM** farther and farther away, a **strong current** made me lose my balance.

"Look up!" Thea shouted.

It was Lucas, the *gigantic* silverix whale we had met during our trip. He had emerged from behind a rock and was now **following** the pirate spaceship!

Unexpected Help

Something *FLASHED* by me. Wait, had I seen that correctly? I looked again. **Martian mozzarella!** Benjamin and Bugsy Wugsy were holding on to Lucas's ꝼin!

The whale reached the pirate's spaceship in three quick tail **flaps**. Then Lucas grabbed the spaceship in his gigantic fangs and shook it from **left** to *right* and *UP* and **down**. I wouldn't have wanted to be in the pirates' fur: They must have been feeling very **SEASICK**!

A moment later . . . *snap!*

The rope that was pulling the trailer with the chest broke, and the pirates' spaceship **took off** at high speed.

I got a glimpse of Black Star's face in the porthole. He was growling aNGRiLY.

Great galaxies! The spacecats were gone! I hoped I never saw those ferocious felines again.

Lucas swam back to us and gently placed the chest in front of me. Then he very DELICATELY lowered Benjamin and Bugsy Wugsy from his fin. The rest of us rushed over to the mouselings, greeting them with ENORMOUSE hugs.

"Well done!" I told them. "How did you do it?"

It happened like this . . .

"We were out playing with some polpyx when we saw the pirates' spaceship, so we hid," Benjamin explained. "When we realized what the spacecats were up to,

Bugsy Wugsy had the idea to ask *Lucas* for his help."

"Amazing!" Sally said.

"Without you two, the **treasure** would have been lost forever!" Thea added. "And thank you, too, Lucas!"

Fiiiiiiiiiiiihhhhh!

The whale let out one of his whistles. Sally's invention translated for us:

"It was my pleasure, spacemice!"

Lucas **waved** good-bye with one fin while Sally helped the *polpyx* get their chest back. We all gathered around the chest and admired the precious cosmostars that glowed so brightly in the dark abyss.

The three wise ones approached me.

"**Captain Stiltonix**, the creatures of

Aquarix City thank you for coming here and helping us find our cosmostars," the first one said.

"They are essential to the **SURVIVAL** of our species!" the second wise one added.

"According to our customs, when another creature finds something of ours, he has the right to keep haLF of it," the third wise one told us.

Trap's eyes lit up **greedily**.

"Oh, that's so kind of you —"

"But of course we **cannot** accept!" I interrupted, finishing my cousin's sentence for him. "We know how important these stars are to you and your planet. They belong here, not with us!"

As we turned to leave, I looked back at Aquarix City: The polpyx's capital was now shining **brightly** thanks to the cosmostars. What a **warm** and **welcoming** place!

Our mission had been a great success!

A New Mission

It seemed as though our **adventure** was coming to an end. But we were all in for a surprise.

"Captain, **look**!" Professor Greenfur called. I approached the pirates' trailer and leaned over to peek inside. I was *astonished*: It was full of other **precious** things that had been **STOLEN** from all over the universe!

"Ohhhhhhh!" Trap gasped. His beady, greedy little eyes *lit* up. "We were looking for **ONE** treasure, but we found **hundreds** of other treasures!"

He draped a golden pearl **necklace** around his neck and cradled a fancy chrome blender in his paws.

"We can take this back to MouseStar 1," he continued. "I'm sure Cook Squizzy could use it for his triple cheese shakes!"

"Put those down, Trap!" Thea scolded him. "I'm sorry to disappoint you, but these objects were STOLEN by the pirates and must be returned to their legitimate owners."

Professor Greenfur nodded.

"I already did a quick estimate, and these objects come from at least seven different galaxies!"

I almost fainted.

You know what that meant, right? It meant that instead of going back to the MouseStar 1, we would be traveling around for days — who am I kidding — for weeks, months, or even YEARS returning those precious things!

But that's an adventure for **another time**, my friends.

See you on the next astral adventure of the spacemice!

Don't miss any adventures of the Spacemice!

#1 Alien Escape

#2 You're Mine, Captain!

#3 Ice Planet Adventure

#4 The Galactic Goal

#5 Rescue Rebellion

#6 The Underwater Planet

#7 Beware! Space Junk!

Be sure to read all my fabumouse adventures!

#1 Lost Treasure of the Emerald Eye

#2 The Curse of the Cheese Pyramid

#3 Cat and Mouse in a Haunted House

#4 I'm Too Fond of My Fur!

#5 Four Mice Deep in the Jungle

#6 Paws Off, Cheddarface!

#7 Red Pizzas for a Blue Count

#8 Attack of the Bandit Cats

#9 A Fabumouse Vacation for Geronimo

#10 All Because of a Cup of Coffee

#11 It's Halloween, You 'Fraidy Mouse!

#12 Merry Christmas, Geronimo!

#13 The Phantom of the Subway

#14 The Temple of the Ruby of Fire

#15 The Mona Mousa Code

#16 A Cheese-Colored Camper

#17 Watch Your Whiskers, Stilton!

#18 Shipwreck on the Pirate Islands

#19 My Name Is Stilton, Geronimo Stilton

#20 Surf's Up, Geronimo!

#21 The Wild, Wild West

#22 The Secret of Cacklefur Castle

A Christmas Tale

#23 Valentine's Day Disaster

#24 Field Trip to Niagara Falls

#25 The Search for Sunken Treasure

#26 The Mummy with No Name

#27 The Christmas Toy Factory

#28 Wedding Crasher

#29 Down and Out Down Under

#30 The Mouse Island Marathon

#31 The Mysterious Cheese Thief

Christmas Catastrophe

#32 Valley of the Giant Skeletons

#33 Geronimo and the Gold Medal Mystery

#34 Geronimo Stilton, Secret Agent

#35 A Very Merry Christmas

#36 Geronimo's Valentine

#37 The Race Across America

#38 A Fabumouse School Adventure

#39 Singing Sensation

#40 The Karate Mouse

#41 Mighty Mount Kilimanjaro

#42 The Peculiar Pumpkin Thief

#43 I'm Not a Supermouse!

#44 The Giant Diamond Robbery

#45 Save the White Whale!

#46 The Haunted Castle

#47 Run for the Hills, Geronimo!

#48 The Mystery in Venice

#49 The Way of the Samurai

#50 This Hotel Is Haunted!

#51 The Enormouse Pearl Heist

#52 Mouse in Space!

#53 Rumble in the Jungle

#54 Get into Gear, Stilton!

#55 The Golden Statue Plot

#56 Flight of the Red Bandit

The Hunt for the Golden Book

#57 The Stinky Cheese Vacation

#58 The Super Chef Contest

#59 Welcome to Moldy Manor

The Hunt for the Curious Cheese

#60 The Treasure of Easter Island

#61 Mouse House Hunter

#62 Mouse Overboard!

The Hunt for the Secret Papyrus

#63 The Cheese Experiment

Join me and my friends as we travel through time in these very special editions!

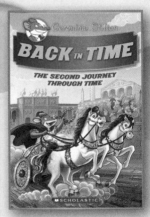

THE JOURNEY THROUGH TIME

BACK IN TIME:
THE SECOND JOURNEY THROUGH TIME

THE RACE AGAINST TIME
THE THIRD JOURNEY THROUGH TIME

Don't miss any of these exciting Thea Sisters adventures!

Thea Stilton and the Dragon's Code

Thea Stilton and the Mountain of Fire

Thea Stilton and the Ghost of the Shipwreck

Thea Stilton and the Secret City

Thea Stilton and the Mystery in Paris

Thea Stilton and the Cherry Blossom Adventure

Thea Stilton and the Star Castaways

Thea Stilton: Big Trouble in the Big Apple

Thea Stilton and the Ice Treasure

Thea Stilton and the Secret of the Old Castle

Thea Stilton and the Blue Scarab Hunt

Thea Stilton and the Prince's Emerald

Thea Stilton and the Mystery on the Orient Express

Thea Stilton and the Dancing Shadows

Thea Stilton and the Legend of the Fire Flowers

Thea Stilton and the Spanish Dance Mission

Thea Stilton and the Journey to the Lion's Den

Thea Stilton and the Great Tulip Heist

Thea Stilton and the Chocolate Sabotage

Thea Stilton and the Missing Myth

Thea Stilton and the Lost Letters

Thea Stilton and the Tropical Treasure

Thea Stilton and the Hollywood Hoax

Meet
GERONIMO STILTONOOT

He is a cavemouse — Geronimo Stilton's ancient ancestor! He runs the stone newspaper in the prehistoric village of Old Mouse City. From dealing with dinosaurs to dodging meteorites, his life in the Stone Age is full of adventure!

#1 The Stone of Fire

#2 Watch Your Tail!

#3 Help, I'm in Hot Lava!

#4 The Fast and the Frozen

#5 The Great Mouse Race

#6 Don't Wake the Dinosaur!

#7 I'm a Scaredy-Mouse!

#8 Surfing for Secrets

#9 Get the Scoop, Geronimo!

#10 My Autosaurus Will Win!

#11 Sea Monster Surprise

Don't miss any of my magical special edition adventures!

THE KINGDOM OF FANTASY

THE QUEST FOR PARADISE:
THE RETURN TO THE KINGDOM OF FANTASY

THE AMAZING VOYAGE:
THE THIRD ADVENTURE IN THE KINGDOM OF FANTASY

THE DRAGON PROPHECY:
THE FOURTH ADVENTURE IN THE KINGDOM OF FANTASY

THE VOLCANO OF FIRE:
THE FIFTH ADVENTURE IN THE KINGDOM OF FANTASY

THE SEARCH FOR TREASURE:
THE SIXTH ADVENTURE IN THE KINGDOM OF FANTASY

THE ENCHANTED CHARMS:
THE SEVENTH ADVENTURE IN THE KINGDOM OF FANTASY

THE PHOENIX OF DESTINY:
AN EPIC KINGDOM OF FANTASY ADVENTURE

THE HOUR OF MAGIC:
THE EIGHTH ADVENTURE IN THE KINGDOM OF FANTASY

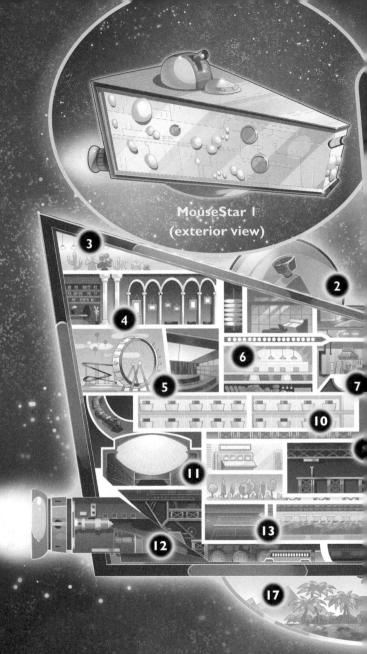

MouseStar 1

The spaceship, home, and refuge of the spacemice!

MouseStar 1
(exterior view)

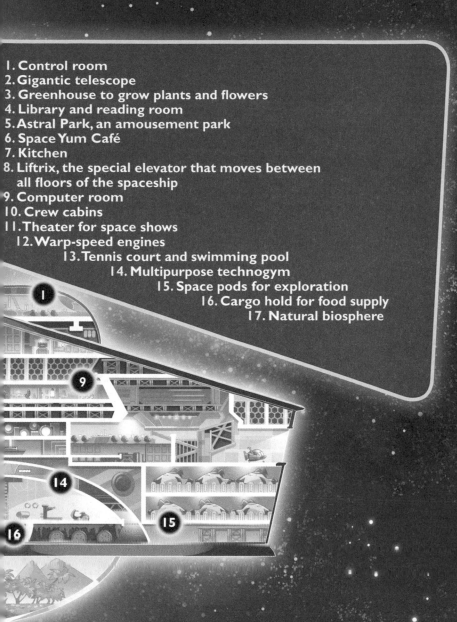

1. Control room
2. Gigantic telescope
3. Greenhouse to grow plants and flowers
4. Library and reading room
5. Astral Park, an amusement park
6. Space Yum Café
7. Kitchen
8. Liftrix, the special elevator that moves between all floors of the spaceship
9. Computer room
10. Crew cabins
11. Theater for space shows
12. Warp-speed engines
13. Tennis court and swimming pool
14. Multipurpose technogym
15. Space pods for exploration
16. Cargo hold for food supply
17. Natural biosphere

*Dear mouse friends,
thanks for reading,
and good-bye until the next book.
See you in outer space!*